The Memory Quilt

WRITTEN AND ILLUSTRATED BY

Elizabeth McKey Hulbert

A WINDSWEPT BOOK

Windswept House
MT. DESERT, MAINE

This book is for
> Bill and Kate and Tom
> Cary and Christopher
> Sarah and Hannah and Jonah

Printed in the United States of America
for the Publisher by
Furbush-Roberts
Bangor, Maine

Ethan came alone to stay with Granma on the island — the island of the pointy green fir trees and loud blue sea ... the island of the marmalade cat and the teasing Roode twins and Uncle Dicky with his big boots and lobster smell ... the island of cobblestone beaches and the round little harbor that Ma and Pa had said perhaps this summer Ethan could row across all by himself.

But this summer they wouldn't be here to tell him yes or no. They wouldn't be here, or anywhere, ever again. Ethan hoped Granma would say something to make him feel better — something warm and funny and loving like old times.

She didn't. She gave Ethan a brief hug, hard and knotty as her hands and said, "What is, is," in such a way that all Ethan's questions stuck in his throat. Her eyes were puffy, as if she'd cried some, but her mouth was a tight, twisty line like an old stick set across her wrinkled face. Uncle Dicky tried to help, carrying the suitcases and boxes that held all Ethan's things up the narrow stairs and patting him awkwardly on the shoulder.

"I'm awful sorry, boy, but we're real glad you're here. Things get settled a bit, we'll have us some good times."

Bed time was bad.

"I'm not sleepy. I want a glass of water. I'm cold."

Granma brought another blanket, plain gray-white and scratchy.

" 'Spose you were used to fancy stuff."

"I had a quilt." Ethan sat up in bed to tell her. "Big and puffy and warm as toast."

"Hmph!"

Ethan cried a while in the sad darkness, and then he climbed down and opened the door so light from downstairs shone in.

In the morning there was something by his breakfast plate — a square of cotton about the size of a handkerchief, covered with soft white puffs that looked like tiny rabbit tails.

"Puffy, you said," Granma told him, thumping down a tall glass of milk. "Clean your plate now. 'Tis a quilt square."

Ethan didn't feel hungry. His plate held a whole mound of food — fried eggs, sausage, two enormous doughnuts.

"I usually just have dry cereal and juice," he murmured. "That's what I eat for breakfast."

"Your Granma's quite a hand at quilt makin'." Uncle Dicky slid one of the eggs over to his own plate. "Better give me one of those doughnuts, too. Yessir, she can sew up a pretty coverlet faster'n you can say 'Clam Pie'!"

He went off, whistling, to his boat.

"Can we go clamming, Granma?" Ethan remembered the muddy flats in the cove, Pa laughing as they dug out the clams, with their long necks stuck way out sometimes, and squirting.

"Clammin' today? No, no, no!" Granma was brisk. "This is wash day. We got to step lively."

She stepped lively, and Ethan, not sure what to do, trailed behind: he was a ghost with the dirty sheets, a turtle with the laundry basket for a shell, birds snapping their beaks as he handed clothespins to Granma.

Finally she snapped, too. "Pity sakes, Ethan! You're more hindrance than help. Skedaddle!"

He spent the rest of the day playing with the marmalade cat.

"My cat at home was black," he said at supper. "I like black cats."

Ethan lay awake in his bed a long, long time. Finally he fell asleep right in the middle of a fuzzy, hurting memory of Ma's voice singing, "Sleep, my cocoon-kin, sleep, sleep ... "

There was another quilt square in the morning, next to the biggest bowl of oatmeal Ethan had ever seen.

"Slosh the syrup onto it, boy," Uncle Dicky whispered, "an' it'll slide down real easy."

The quilt square Granma had made was a black cat, cut a mite crudely, but sitting up straight and proud on a flowered calico background. It looked a lot like Ethan's old cat.

Ethan tried to tell her so, but the hot, thick oatmeal stuck in his throat and he choked and choked.

"Down your Sunday throat, eh?" Uncle Dicky pounded him on the back and Granma hurried for water.

"Is it Sunday?" Sundays used to be fun. "Can we go on a picnic?" Ethan remembered a beach where the rocks were round and smooth, pretty-colored — black, white, orange, speckled like birds' eggs. "Can we go rowing?" The harbor was sparkling; Uncle Dicky's boat bobbed up and down.

"Sunday throat's just an ol' sayin'." Granma bustled around the flour bin. "This is bakin' day."

Baking day wasn't any better for Ethan than wash day had been. His lump of dough plopped to the floor when he tried to knead it as Granma was doing, and his piece of pie crust wrapped itself around the rolling pin. Granma shooed him outdoors finally, and he sat on the bulkhead watching the crows and gulls flying across the shore meadow. They swooped back and forth, crying harshly, dropping shellfish to break on the rocks where the waves curled in. The birds looked beautiful against the blue sky ... so white and so black. Watching made Ethan feel very lonely.

"Come, Granma," he called. "Come watch with me."

But she stayed busy in the house, and he sat alone a long time, until the birds flew off to their night perches and the marmalade cat came meowing for his supper.

At bed time Ethan's door was left ajar. Through it he heard Granma's voice, loud and sorrowful, "Dumbed birds! A-squawkin' all day, an' the boy just a-settin' there. Lookin' at him I get to rememberin' ... an' it's like to drive me crazy. I dunno just what I'm goin' to do!" And he heard also a bit of Uncle Dicky's low answer, "I dunno, either, Mother. But don't you go turnin' bitter, now. No sir, don't you be a bitter ol' woman ... "

The morning's quilt square was a gull, cloud white, and a crow, glossy black sateen, against a sky blue background. Granma must have worked real late to get them sewed.

She must have watched the crows and gulls herself from the kitchen window. Probably it would have driven her crazy to watch outside with him.

Ethan's stomach did a crazy flip-flop. Breakfast was codfish gravy over potatoes, salty and hot and smelling strong. He pushed his plate away. "I don't want that!" He stared hard at Granma and then he pushed the quilt square onto the floor. "I don't want that either!"

He slid out of his chair and slammed out of the kitchen door. Uncle Dicky caught up with him by the porch steps.

"I got to get somethin' over to the store," he said. "Whyn't you come along an' mebbe we can get some of that dry cereal you said you liked."

They walked steadily, side by side, and were almost around the curve of the harbor before Uncle Dicky spoke again. "You an' your Granma got to be patient with each other, I guess. Folks got different ways of servin' sorrow." He looked uncomfortable, and before Ethan could think of anything to say, Uncle Dicky began talking quickly about the harbor. "Got to be careful ... there's a real nasty current sweeps through here at tide change ... "

At the store fat Mag smiled widely at Uncle Dicky as she waited on him, and gave Ethan three free licorice sticks along with the cereal.

"My, my," she said, wagging her head, "if you don't 'mind me of your pa. Walk just like him, you do. Got your ma's yellow hair, all right, but you're the spittin' image of him!"

Ethan walked tall and careful all the way back to the house. He wished Granma had heard what Mag said. Maybe she'd look out the window and see him coming just like Pa ... and then he'd do something patient and she'd like that.

Granma was already out in her vegetable garden, scrunched down and yanking up weeds.

"You can start at the other end," she called over her shoulder, not looking.

Halfway down the second row Ethan had to speak out. "She wasn't, you know!"

"What? Who wasn't what?"

"My mother wasn't going too fast. The other car crossed the line."

"Mmmphmmm, that's what they said."

There was a long pause, and then Granma stood up shakily, peering down the length of garden. Her voice changed. "Great land, boy! You've gone an' pulled up all the spinach an' left the weeds!"

So gardening day wasn't any better than wash day and baking day had been ... or the next few days were. There weren't any more quilt squares at the breakfast table. Granma buzzed around, busy as ever, but her face looked pinched and bitter. Uncle Dicky spent the time in his fish house, mending traps. Ethan felt unnecessary and desperate.

Then there came a rainy day and they went up-attic to clean.

"Cultch!" Granma snorted at the mess of boxes and trunks and old furniture, the mouse sign and cobwebs. That must mean something bad, Ethan thought, way she said it, and the dim room under the eaves was dirty, piled with stuff every which-way. But it was private and peaceful and they did find something wonderful: stored away carefully amidst the dusty clutter were the old toys that Uncle Dicky and Ethan's father had played with.

"Oh!" Granma's voice was stiff. "It's your pa's ol' rockin' horse ..." She paused and then the words tumbled out as if she couldn't help it. "Why, I remember, days like this, he'd rock an' rock ... always the same game he'd play, yes, always the same one: he'd ride clear off-island ... away off to Bangor an' back ... "

Ethan climbed on, cobwebs and all. The horse was a mite small for him, but the narrow wooden seat felt firm under his rear, the cracked leather reins were still in one piece.

"Hey! My Pa's horse. Hey, hey!"

He rode and rode — long after Granma had gone back downstairs. He rode all around the island, even the wild wood-roads in the middle — just as his Pa had done. He didn't know what Bangor was, but he even rode there, too.

"Yes, yes, I remember that!" Uncle Dicky laughed out loud. "An' I had a donkey."

But Granma would say nothing more about the toys; she made a great deal of noise washing up the dishes, and then sat at her sewing table.

Ethan dreamed of the horse that night: the horse was covered with quilt squares of every rainbow color, and he rode it through the clouds and over the world to find Ma and Pa and let them know that he was all right and going to be happy again.

He woke up feeling tired and eager. As soon as Uncle Dicky left for his fish house, Ethan asked Granma, "Can I bring the horse down here? I can stable him next to the bookcase ... "

"Why no," she said flatly. "That wouldn't do at all. I wouldn't want to see it there. No."

Suddenly it was all too much for Ethan. Something snapped inside him. He ran to the sewing table and kicked it, sending the finished quilt squares and snippets of material flying.

"I hate it," he screamed. "I hate you. You're a — a bitter ol' woman, and you don't want my Pa's horse and you don't want me. You just want your ol' sewing. I hate it and I hate you!"

Wildly he flung himself out of the house and tore through the meadow, towards the shore woods. He spent a long time sprawled on the moss under a huge fir where he and his parents had picnicked in that sweet and terrible time that would never come again. He cried and yelled and pounded the pricky-soft ground, and after a while he felt better.

He heard the sound of oars plashing and came out of the woods to investigate. The Roode twins, in a battered dory, were pulling into the shore.

"Well, hunh," they called, sighting him. "We been away. We just heard you was here an' come to see if your granny would let you play."

The old taunting, sneering note made Ethan reckless.

"I can do anything I want," he said loudly. "Now."

"Yeah, that's right." Liburti was the fatter one. "Now you're a norfan."

"Yeah," Selsus echoed. "We come to see what a norfan looks like."

They laughed meanly and poked each other.

"Hey! I wonder if norfans can row? Can you row?"

Pa had been teaching him, past summers, and two days ago Uncle Dicky had let him row out to the *Marianna B.*

"Sure," said Ethan.

"All right." Selsus gestered. "You can row our boat back acrost an' we'll see if norfans row as good as us."

"C'mon norfan." Liburti was the meaner. "Or would Granny mind somethin' awful?"

"She wouldn't care."

She probably wouldn't even notice. Ethan walked to the dory. The twins held it for him to get in and set the oars, and then pushed him off, making remarks as he struggled to point the boat's bow at the town wharf across the harbor.

"We'll get there afore you," they catcalled, beginning to run.

Near shore it wasn't bad going. The dory was a heavy old thing, but Ethan set his toes and his shoulders, and anger and a kind of hopeless desperation kept him pulling hard at the big, unwieldy oars. He got almost halfway across without any trouble. Then he became aware that the tide was changing — and the fierce current, Uncle Dicky had mentioned, pulled devilishly at the boat. The water around him was blue-green and fast, frothing and churning, with swirlings and suckings that had a strength all their own. Ethan could see the lobster buoys set near the harbor's rocky mouth strain and pull, their cork bobbins wrenched under by the tide's force.

He pulled on the oars with all his strength — and the boat didn't move at all, then wavered and pointed for an awful moment straight out the channel to open sea. He heard a shout and, giving a shoreward glance, saw figures running along the water's edge. The Roodes, Liburti and Selsus, of course, but two others ... one big, striding longly, the other little and darting. Uncle Dicky and Granma!

Ethan bent to his oars, remembering the short, strong fisherman's chop that Uncle Dicky used. He passed the *Marianna B.*, swinging at her mooring almost in center harbor, and then, with kelp swirling heavily past his stern, pulled into the quieter water that lay brown and faintly rippled to the end of the town wharf.

"What the ... !" Uncle Dicky secured the painter, grabbed Ethan ashore. The Roode twins seemed to have evaporated, but Granma trotted up almost at once, panting and distraught.

"What's this foolishness!" She grabbed Ethan's hand and held it tightly. "I like to died when I looked over an' saw you swivitin' 'cross harbor in that ol' dory, with the tide runnin' hard!"

"The Roode twins made me. They called me a norfan!" Ethan heard his voice sounding quite wild. "They said if you're a norfan you don't have anyone really cares. And you're always busy ... and sewing ... and I can't even weed right ... and, and ... they made me row!"

"Hmph. Takes willin' feet to tramp up fool's hill. Howsomever, Roode's their name an' rude's their manners!"

"Norfan?" Uncle Dicky looked bewildered for a moment. "Oh, orphan! You're no orphan, boy. An orphan's got no one to love 'em an' care. You got your granma an' you got me."

He took Ethan's other hand and they walked back around the shore that way, three abreast. Starting up through the shore meadow, Ethan finally spoke.

"I did do it, though, didn't I? I rowed across the harbor all by myself."

"Yep, you did." Uncle Dicky grinned down at him. "An' that was some wicked good rowin', too."

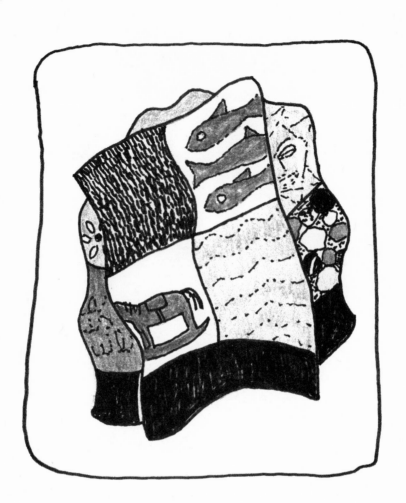

"I guess," said Granma, as they entered the house, "that I'd best tell you about the quilt, seein's how you got the wrong idea. I thought it might help you keep your memories, boy, whilst keepin' you warm ... but 'tain't quite finished ... "

The quilt squares were all pieced together, ready to be slipped over the thicker lining. Some needed the final stitches.

"Your granma ain't much for rememberin' with words," Uncle Dicky added. "She thought you'd like this."

"It's for me. My own memory quilt!"

Ethan liked it so much he stood still and looked and looked.

There was the puffy white square. There was his black cat, sitting proud. There was a piece of strong blue, like the color of his pa's eyes, and a laughing golden yellow one like his ma's hair. There were the crow and gull, and next to it a plain black, deep furry velvet like sorrow or anger. There was even a square with little green plants sewn onto it. Spinach! And a lovely dark green of the pointy firs. There was a silvery gray like the fog that sometimes wrapped the island silent and secret, and a checkered gingham piece with three silver fishes laid on like the inside of a fancy picnic basket. There was the rocking horse, the Roode twins in outline (Selsus in black corduroy and Liburti in blue denim), and a clever square of mixed rounds, like stones on the beach. There was the *Marianna B.* for Uncle Dicky, and a square with Granma's initials and the date, and one that said, "Ethan, his Quilt," embroidered neat and clear.

That night Ethan slept under the memory quilt. Granma came up and tucked him in.

"There now," she said, perching for a moment on his bed. "You're snug's a bug in a rug. Sleep tight."

Snug's a bug in a rug. Cocoon-kin.

Well, they're near the same thing.

Ethan slept, smiling.

ABOUT THE AUTHOR

Elizabeth McKey Hulbert is an artist and author who has worked in the editorial, advertising, and museum fields. She has written several books for children (*I Love to Ski*, Windswept, 1986), and articles for magazines and newspapers on many subjects. She enjoys gardening, cooking, sailing, books, hiking, and tennis. Manset, on Mt. Desert Island, Maine, is her home.